W9-AUD-365

YOUNG EXPLORERS

THE MISSING NECKLACE

Place SUCCESS BADGE here! Read page 73 to learn how to get it.

SOLVED

Written by B. Vitale and J. I. Wagner. Illustrated by J. G. Ratti. Edited by T. Phua.

All rights reserved. Copyright 2020 by J. I. Wagner. Published by freshabooks. freshabooks is an imprint of: freshamedia GmbH, Robert-Bosch-Str. 32, 63303 Dreieich, Germany.

www.timmitobbson.com | www.freshabooks.com

ISBN 978-3-96326-737-6

Printed 2021 in the United States of America.

Certified Chain of Custody
Promoting Sustainable Forestry
www.sfiprogram.org
SFI-01268

SUSTAINABLE FORESTRY INITIATIVE

SFI label applies to the text stock

Hi. I'm Timmi.

I may not be the most confident boy. Or the most athletic. Or the best at anything. But I *am* quite curious. That seems to be good.

This is Lilli.

She can be stubborn. And sassy. But above all, she is the bravest and boldest person I know. She'd do anything to help you.

This is Marvin.

He loves animals. Whenever he gets excited, he bobs up and down on the spot. And he claps. It looks silly, but he doesn't care.

The Young Explorers

This is our own little club. We want to help others and train to one day get accepted as students at Backalley One.

Pssst. Here is a secret mission. The seven images to the right can each be found on the following pages! Search for them and note the page number you found them on. Then go to timmitobbson.com and find the secret area. Enter the page numbers to pass the security check. A surprise awaits you!

Backalley One

A secret club for great adventurers and detectives who solve mysteries no one else can. We recently found its hidden location.

This is Boris.

Boris is the head of Backalley One. We only met him once. He accepted us as early apprentices and told us we would hear from him once we were ready. We are waiting.

This is Tom.

Unbelievable. My older brother is a student at Backalley One! He works with Boris. How could I not have noticed?

This is the story of how we solved our first mystery as the **Young Explorers**.

Find:

Found
on page:

THE MISSING NECKLACE

FACTS
FOR EXPLORERS

HANDBOOK
FOR EXPLORERS

MISSING

It was still early morning when I walked up the path to school. The sky was blue. Birds were chirping. It was going to be a beautiful day. Or so I thought. Then I spotted Lilli and Marvin. They were reading a newspaper.

"Timmi," Marvin said. "Come quick!"

"What is it?" I asked.

"Someone is stealing jewelry . . . in public and in broad daylight. Twenty thefts were reported yesterday. Twenty!"

"Wow!" I said. "In just one day? The police have no clues?"

"No," Lilli said. "No one has seen the thief. The papers are calling him *invisible*."

"This could be a case for the Young Explorers," Marvin said. "The thief is invisible. It's a mystery! It's perfect!"

"Yes, you're right," I said. "If we solve this case, I bet Backalley One will let us help with one of their mysteries!"

Lilli pointed at my shirt. "Speaking of mysteries . . . what happened?"

"Oh, no," I said, noticing the stain on my shirt. "I went to the park on my way here."

"And played in the mud?" she asked.

"I slipped and fell near a bench," I said.

"Anyway, are you ready for our presentations?" I asked, trying to avoid talking more about my muddy shirt.

It was family day at school. We each had to show something important to our families.

Lilli nodded. "I have Grandpa's watch."

"I brought our family tree," Marvin said. "What did you bring?"

"A necklace that has been in our family for centuries," I said. "Here's an old picture of Grandma wearing it!"

Lilli looked at the photo. "Wow. It's pretty. Did you bring the real necklace?"

I nodded and reached back into my bag.

There was nothing there. It was missing!

"Maybe the Invisible Thief took it,"

Marvin said, his eyes growing wide.

"It must have fallen out when I slipped

in the park!" I said, my voice trembling.

"Or . . ." Marvin said, "the thief took it!"

Lilli punched Marvin on the shoulder.

"Don't worry, Timmi. We'll find it," she said.

My friends and I ran back to the park.

"Where did you fall?" Marvin asked.

"I don't know exactly. In a mud puddle

near a bench," I said. I could feel my heart

pounding. There were so many benches!

"There was a little sign on the backrest of the bench," I said. "And it was next to a trash can."

"Good," Lilli said. "Anything else?"

"Yes," I said nervously. "My mom is going to be so mad at me."

"That's not helping," Lilli said.

I nodded. "There were two trees nearby."

The three of us looked around.

"I see two benches that fit your description," Lilli said.

"I know which one it is," Marvin said.

> The solution to each puzzle is revealed at the beginning of the following chapter.
> You can find hints at the back of this book.

Next to which bench did Timmi slip and fall?

BAD LUCK

Marvin ran to the bench in the far left
corner of the park. "This is it!"

"How do you know it's not that one?"
Lilli asked, pointing. "It matches what
Timmi told us, too."

16

"True," Marvin said. "But this is the only bench with a mud puddle near it. Just like the one Timmi fell in!"

"He's right," I said. "This is where it happened."

Lilli dropped to the ground. "Then the necklace must be here. Let's look!"

Suddenly, I spied something shiny under the bench. I reached for it, certain it was the necklace.

But it was just a piece of wrapper.

Disappointed, I pulled my head out from under the bench.

But I did not pull it out far enough.

"Ouch!" I said as I bumped my head.

"You okay?" Lilli asked. "That sounded like it hurt."

I rubbed my head. It was a bit sore, but I was okay.

Just then I started to laugh.

"What's so funny?" Lilli asked.

"My grandma," I said.

Lilli and Marvin looked at each other.

"I don't get it," Marvin said.

"She calls it her good-luck necklace," I said.

"She told me once that bad things would happen if it wasn't with someone in the family. If she were here, I know just what she'd say. She would tell me I bumped my head because I lost the necklace."

"Wow, a real good-luck charm!" Lilli said. "Do you think she's right?"

"No way," I said. "I love my grandma, but good luck? Bad luck? There's no such thing. I bumped my head because I was crawling under a bench!"

"I don't know," Marvin said. "Your grandma *is* ninety-one. She must have *some* kind of luck on her side."

Before I could answer, we heard a shout.

"Help!" A woman ran toward us.

"Someone stole one of my bracelets!"

Lilli tried to calm the woman. "Maybe we can help. Did you see the thief?"

"I felt a tug on my arm," she said. "But when I turned, no one was there."

"The Invisible Thief!" Marvin said. "What did the bracelet look like?"

"Just like the other one I'm wearing. Ruby red with big green jewels," she said. "Ruby red bracelets are very in right now. Everyone is wearing them."

Lilli snorted.

"Just look over there," the woman said.

"Wow! You're right," Lilli said, glancing at the street behind the park.

"Most come with fake jewels. But the ones on mine are real and valuable!"

"Hold on. I think I see yours!" I shouted.

Can you spot a bracelet with green jewels?

Parkside Fashion

FOLLOW THE THIEF

"See the pigeon flying over the bus stop?" I shouted. "It's carrying a bracelet with green jewels!"

"You've got to be kidding," Lilli said.

"Doves can be trained," Marvin said.

"Come on. Let's see where it's going."

Lilli, Marvin, and I raced out of the park.

Eyes to the sky, we followed the bird.

After several minutes of running, we

suddenly lost sight of it.

"Where did it go?" I shouted.

We searched the sky.

"There!" Lilli said.

The bird landed on the roof of a house

protected by a tall wall.

"Where are we?" I asked, taking a puff

from my inhaler.

Lilli shook her head. "I don't know.

Somewhere at the edge of town."

"I've never been here before," said

Marvin. "This house looks scary."

I nodded. "I bet no one has lived here

for a long time."

As we watched, the bird flapped its wings and disappeared through an open window.

"Did you see that?" Lilli said. "It flew inside!"

"I bet the bird steals jewelry and delivers the loot to this place!" Marvin shouted.

"No way. Birds don't deliver stuff," I said.

"They can be trained," he said. "Ever heard of homing pigeons?"

I hadn't. But I believed Marvin.

Taking a deep breath, I grabbed a vine hanging on the wall.

"That means we go in?" I asked.

My friends nodded and I started climbing.

I was halfway up when the vine broke.
I fell, scraping my knee against the
bricks.

"Ouch!" I shouted.

"You okay?" Lilli asked for the second
time that day.

I nodded, trying to hold back tears.

"Maybe that necklace *is* good luck, after all," Marvin said. "Look at what's happened since you lost it. You fell in the mud. You hit your head. And now you've scraped your knee."

I shook my head. "There's no such thing as bad luck. Come on."

Using the vines and cracks in the wall, we started to climb.

"Whoa," I said when I got to the top.

"What?" Lilli asked.

Then she saw it. On the other side of the wall were bushes as far as the eye could see.

Lilli grinned. "It's a maze. Let's go!"

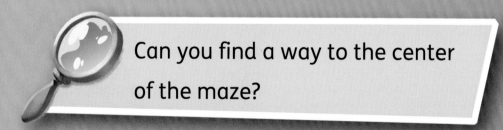

Can you find a way to the center of the maze?

The starting point is at the bottom.

NOBODY'S HOME

Stepping out of the maze, I looked up at the house. It really was in bad shape.

"It's like the house was just forgotten," I said.

Marvin pressed his face up to a window. "Looks like no one has been here in a long time."

"But the bird is in there for sure. What if it stole my grandma's necklace and brought it here too?" I asked. "It will break her heart if I don't bring it home with me. I have to go in."

I put my hand on the doorknob.

"Are you sure about this?" Marvin asked.

He bobbed up and down nervously. "If

bad luck is following you, going in might

not be the best idea."

Marvin was right. For all we knew, we were heading into a thief's hideout. But I felt like I had no choice.

I turned the knob. The door opened with a loud creak.

Inside, the furniture was covered by sheets. There were cobwebs and dust everywhere. It felt spooky.

We slowly crept through the house, searching each room. In the kitchen, Marvin opened the fridge.

"Ugh, gross!" he whispered, and closed it quickly.

A horrible smell wafted into the room.

"Hey, look," I said pointing to the ground.

There was a deep rut in the kitchen floor. It started at a cabinet and went in a semicircle. Slowly, I pulled at the cabinet. It swung open, revealing a narrow, dimly lit corridor.

"A secret passage!" I said, my eyes growing wide.

"I bet this leads to the stolen jewelry," Marvin said, quietly clapping his hands.

"Guys, wait!" Lilli said.

"What is it?" I asked.

"I think someone has been here. In this kitchen. And very recently!" she whispered.

What did Lilli notice?

A THIEF'S HIDEOUT

"Look," Lilli said. "The teapot is still hot. There is steam coming from it. Whoever was here could come back any moment!"

Right then, we heard the loud creak of the entrance door.

"In here," I said, waving the others on.

We dashed into the secret passage, closing the cabinet behind us. After squeezing through the narrow corridor, we came out into a hidden room.

"Hey, look! Birds!" Marvin said. "Lots!"

Lilli stepped closer. "Homing pigeons," she said. "Just like you said, Marvin."

PLASTIC

"People train homing pigeons to deliver notes," Marvin said. "The birds do their job and then come home."

"But these birds aren't bringing home notes," I said. "They're bringing home jewelry."

REAL!!!

Lilli nodded. "So it seems."

"Here," Marvin called. "Look at this!"

Marvin was standing in front of a pile
of jewelry. There were a lot of rings and
bracelets. But my grandma's necklace
was nowhere to be seen.

47

We looked into each of the cages.
The bracelet that had been stolen from the woman in the park was easy to find. The pigeon had placed it right in front of the cage door. But none of the other cages had any jewelry in them.

I was starting to think my grandma was right. Without that charm, bad things *did* happen. First the mud. Then my head and knee. And now we couldn't find Grandma's necklace, although it had to be here somewhere.

"Let's search the rest of this room," Lilli suggested.

"No, we need to get out of here," I told my friends. "The thief could come in any second. He must not know his hideout has been discovered."

"I think he'll know, anyway," Lilli said.
"Too many things have been moved
around. If we don't put them back, the
thief will notice someone was in here."

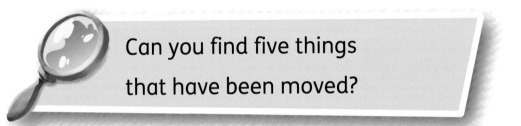

Can you find five things
that have been moved?

DETECTIVE MARVIN

"I think we moved the book, the pencil, the chair, the rug and that tool from the workbench," Lilli said. "Let's put those back in place."

Suddenly we heard footsteps.

They came from the secret passage.

"Quick," I whispered. We all climbed

onto the table and threw the window

open. Just as we were jumping out, a

man entered the hideout. He looked at

us, completely puzzled.

"Go!" I shouted.

We raced through the maze and made it back to the street.

"We have to tell the police," I panted.

Lilli and Marvin nodded. Together, we walked to the police station.

"How can I help?" a detective asked.

"We were at the park today," I said. "A bird stole a bracelet."

"We followed the bird to an old house," Lilli added. "And found a lot of jewelry!"

"And homing pigeons," Marvin said.

"Homing pigeons," the detective said.

"That's new. Could you find the house again?"

Lilli, Marvin, and I nodded.

"That's great news," he said. "You know, you kids may have just solved the case of the Invisible Thief!"

"We think we saw the thief," Marvin

said.

The detective smiled. "We have a group

of suspects, but no proof. Could you pick

the man out of a picture?"

"For sure," Marvin said, clapping his

hands and bobbing up and down.

The detective took us to a room where he laid out a few pictures.

"This is a gang of thieves called The Nine Twins," he said. "Strange name, I know. Doesn't really make sense. But they sure do look alike. The gang has recently been seen around here."

"It was definitely one of them," Lilli said. "But which one?"

Marvin grinned. He pointed to a picture. "That's your guy," he said. "It was him we saw."

Which portrait was Marvin pointing at?

FOUND

"I'll never forget his face," Marvin said.

"He had two different colored eyes.

They were brown and green. And he had

that scar over his left eyebrow."

The detective smiled. "Well done, kid."

Marvin smiled back. "Thanks!"

"Now, about that house," the detective

said.

I grinned. This time I could help. I am great with directions.

The detective listened and took notes.

"Thanks," he said. "We'll send our men down there right now."

"That's it," I said a few minutes later. "We cracked the case, but Grandma's necklace is still missing. I will have to tell my mom I lost it."

"Well," Marvin said. "It's easier to deliver bad news with your friends at your side."

"Yes, we'll come with you," Lilli said.

At home, we found Mom in the living room.

"What's wrong?" she asked when she saw our sad faces.

Beside me, Lilli put her hand on my shoulder. I could do this.

"It's Grandma's necklace," I said finally.
"It's gone. It must have fallen out of
my bag. I'm so sorry, Mom. We looked
everywhere. And without that necklace
to keep us safe, who knows what bad
things will happen."

Mom looked puzzled.

Then she smiled. "Timmi, Grandma's necklace is not the reason why good or bad things happen."

"But Grandma said . . ." I started to say.

Mom shook her head. "She made that up because you wouldn't stop asking why she wore the necklace!"

"And you didn't lose it," Mom said. "You forgot to take it! It's still in the kitchen."

I couldn't believe it. Jumping up, I raced into the kitchen and nearly bumped into my older brother Tom. He had just hung up the phone.

"That was the police," he said. "They found the Invisible Thief—thanks to you three, it seems?"

I nodded, not sure if he was upset.

"I'm proud of you. The Young Explorers solved their first real case," he said. "I'll report this to Boris at Backalley One. We have a mystery we could use some help with."

"But here is one last test," Tom said.
"Find Grandma's necklace. I spied
it on the counter a minute ago and
hid it away," he said, looking at us
expectantly. "Here are your three clues:

"I have no thirst, but liquid you give me.

"I have no lid, but you like to lift me.

"I have no mouth, but you often kiss me."

Where did Tom hide the necklace?

I fished the necklace out of the mug.

"That was a tough riddle," Marvin said.

Tom grinned. "That was just a warmup.

You haven't seen anything yet! Now hurry

up and go give your presentation."

Now I really had a story to tell! But I was even more excited by what Tom had said. *You haven't seen anything yet.* The Young Explorers were about to get going, and I couldn't wait!

THE END (FOR NOW)

The students at Backalley One strive to solve mysteries, ancient and modern. To be successful, they need to know a lot. Here is a collection of fascinating facts taught at Backalley One that relate to this book's adventure.

Pssst. Get this book's Success Badge!

Collect all the letters displayed in the emblems on the following pages. Rearrange the letters to form two words. Then enter the words in the "Badges" section on timmitobbson.com to download your Success Badge. Print it out and paste it in its place on the first page to show you solved every mystery and read all the facts and tips for young explorers!

For more than three thousand years, people have been using pigeons to deliver secret messages. To do so, a small piece of paper is wrapped around the bird's leg. Once the message is attached, the homing pigeon is set free to fly back home.

Throughout history, these messages have decided the fate of many battles.

In recent years, pigeons have also been used by criminals to deliver larger objects. For example, a pigeon was once caught delivering a cell phone to an inmate in a prison courtyard!

Some birds just like to scoop up pieces of food, but others are actually known for stealing shiny objects and taking them back to their nests! Among these "thieving" birds are bowerbirds, black kites, and bald eagles, to name a few. Scientists believe these birds collect shiny items to impress fellow birds or scare away nest intruders. Although there are no known cases of a bird really stealing jewelry like a pickpocket, there is a young girl in Seattle who actually gets "gifts" from crows she feeds. (True story!)

Who wouldn't want to become invisible once in a while? In fact, the idea of invisibility dates back to the Middle Ages with King Arthur, who allegedly had an invisibility cloak. But will there ever be a way to become invisible in real life? Researchers around the world have been trying different techniques, such as routing light around objects so that it seems as if nothing is there (look up

"Rochester Cloak"). Others have developed a skin—or shield—that reflects light in a way that makes the object beneath appear invisible (look up "Invisibility Shield"). But so far, no true invisibility has been achieved.

How often have you watched a movie or read a book in which someone vanishes behind a portrait, bookshelf, or wall? This might seem made up, but hidden doors really do exist.

The ancient Egyptians were among the first to use secret doors thousands of years ago. In more modern times, the infamous Chicago gangster Al Capone was known to have hidden rooms and passages in his home. He used them to escape from police.

Pickpockets can get very creative when it comes to swiping little objects from their victims—and they do not need animals to do it for them. They often work in teams. One partner distracts the victim, while the other picks the victim's pocket. The very best of them can even steal a watch someone is wearing around their wrist or the belt from a pair of pants without the owner noticing.

Young apprentices get the classified Backalley One Handbook. Now *you* can apply its secrets and become a Young Explorer!

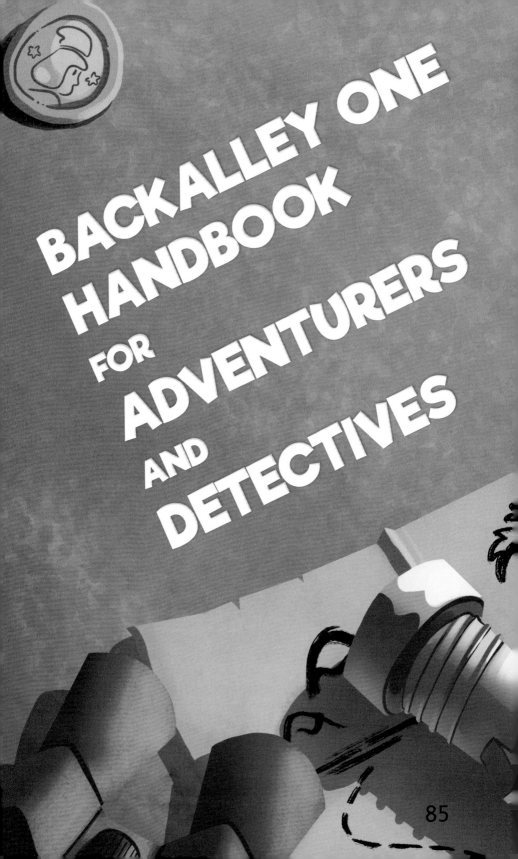

BACKALLEY ONE
HANDBOOK
FOR
ADVENTURERS
AND
DETECTIVES

Solving a case often comes down to the testimony of witnesses.

You can improve your own observation skills with practice! Observe your family or your classmates. Then, without looking at them, list as many of their visual traits as you can remember.

A detailed description might include:

- height
- hair color and style
- eye color
- skin color
- clothes (also shoes)
- body type and size
- glasses
- beard or facial hair
- tattoos or scars
- age
- voice or dialect

This list will also help you when you are questioning witnesses. Use it to guide them toward remembering the important details.

ADVENTURE SKILLS

h

★

SECRET HIDING SPOTS

★

If you want to hide a small object (like a necklace), try the following. You need an empty matchbox and tape. Find a good hiding spot that is safe from prying eyes.

It should also be safe from vacuum cleaners and other cleaning utensils. Use a long strip of tape to stick the matchbox there. Then back up and check to make sure it's not visible.

Is there anything worse than losing something small in a BIG area? If you need to search a huge space and don't know where to look, try walking in a circle around the outside of the area.

Each time you reach your starting point, take one step toward the middle of the area and make another circle. One more way to search is by walking in lines. First walk in one direction, then walk back in the other direction until you have walked the whole area.

Thieves will try to find easy opportunities. Know what they are looking for so you can keep from becoming a target!

- Store your valuables in your front pocket. Pickpockets like to strike from behind.

- Pickpockets love to approach their victims when there are many others around.

A crowd is an excellent distraction. If you are in a busy place, be extra careful.

- If a stranger starts talking to you, be aware of your surroundings and your body! Don't let them touch you. Don't let them distract you so their partner can pickpocket you.

Have you ever been lost inside a maze? Good news. There is a simple way to find your way out. Touch the wall or hedge with one of your hands. Then begin walking, keeping your same hand touching the wall.

If you keep your hand on the wall the whole time, you should find your way out of most maze layouts. The only exception is: if the segment you are touching is a loop. To find out, mark your starting point! If you come back to that point, you will need to touch a different wall and repeat the process.

Pssst. Here are some hints!

 page 15 Marvin listened to what Timmi remembered and then ruled out the benches that didn't fit. Two benches fit the description. Do you see something near one of these two benches that makes it the more likely choice?

 page 25 Think about how the woman described the bracelet. Do you see one that looks like that? Also search in unlikely places.

 page 34 To find the way to the center, you could try the Adventure Skills tip on the previous page. It will take a long time but it will get you to the center.

 page 42 What might be in the kitchen that would show someone has been there recently? Think hot and cold.

 page 51 The kids moved five things around. What did each of them touch? Also check the floor and furniture.

page 58 Marvin noticed something about the thief when the man burst into his lair. What distinguishing features did the man have?

 page 69 Take a look at the illustration and see if you can find an item that fits all three of Tom's clues. Here is a fourth one: I gain weight fast and lose it in gulps.